This book belongs to:

....

Contents

Dentist Trip

Scrub! Scrub! Scrub!

3

"George, are your teeth as clean as mine?" Peppa asks, showing off her clean white teeth.

4

"You both have lovely clean teeth. I'm sure the dentist will be happy!" calls out Daddy Pig.

Later that day, Peppa and George are at the dentists, waiting for their check-up. It is George's first visit.

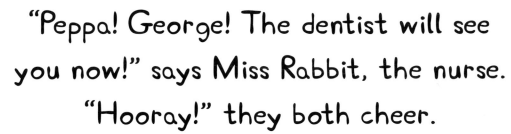

"Peppa! George! The dentist will see you now!" says Miss Rabbit, the nurse. "Hooray!" they both cheer.

This is Doctor Elephant, the dentist. "Who's first?" he asks.

8

"I'm first," replies Peppa.
"I'm a big girl.
Watch me, George!"

9

"Open wide, please!" orders
Doctor Elephant, softly.
"Aaaaah . . ." Peppa opens her mouth
as wide as she possibly can.
"Let's take a look!" says the dentist,
checking Peppa's teeth with a mirror.

"There. All done! What lovely clean teeth!" cheers Doctor Elephant. "Now, you can have the special drink." Gargle! Ptooou! Peppa spits the pink liquid out into the sink. It's George's turn next.

George does not want it to be his turn. So the dentist lets him hold Mr Dinosaur. "All done. You have very strong, clean teeth, George!" smiles Doctor Elephant.

"But wait, what is this?" cries Doctor Elephant. "George has clean teeth, but this young dinosaur's teeth are very dirty."

"Pink!" cries George, picking up a glass. "That's right, George!" says the dentist. "Mr Dinosaur needs some special pink drink!" Gurgle! Gurgle!

George loves Mr Dinosaur. Especially now that he has nice clean teeth.

Nature Trail

Peppa and her family are going on a nature trail. Mummy Pig asks Daddy Pig not to forget the picnic. "As if I would," laughs Daddy Pig.

They head off along the
trail with their map.
Oh dear! Daddy Pig has left
the picnic in the car.

Mummy and Daddy Pig ask Peppa if she can see anything interesting in the forest.
"I don't see anything but boring trees," says Peppa.
Then, she looks really hard and finds some footprints on the ground.

"Let's follow the footprints and see who made them," says Mummy Pig.
"We will have to be very quiet so we don't scare anything away. Shhhh!"

Peppa and George follow the footprints along the ground.
"It looks like they were made by a little bird," says Mummy Pig.

33

Soon, they come to the
end of the footprints.
"The bird has flown up into
that tree," smiles Daddy Pig.

"Where?" asks Peppa.
Daddy Pig gives Peppa binoculars
to help her see the bird.

35

36

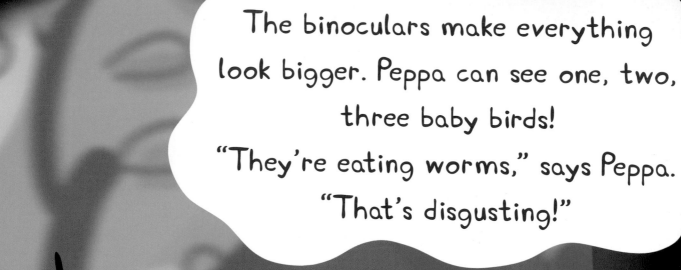

The binoculars make everything look bigger. Peppa can see one, two, three baby birds!
"They're eating worms," says Peppa. "That's disgusting!"

Chirp!

George finds some more footprints. They
are very little. Daddy Pig says they belong
to ants collecting leaves to eat.

"I think it's time for lunch," says Mummy Pig. But Daddy Pig has left the picnic in the car!

40

"My map is wrong," begins Daddy Pig.
"We'll have to follow our own
footprints back to the car."

"Ducks love picnics," says Peppa. "Mrs Duck, can you help us find our picnic please?"

43

The ducks lead Peppa and her family back to their car. "We're here! Thank you for your help Mrs Duck," cries Peppa.

"I love picnics!" laughs Daddy Pig.
The ducks love picnics too.
Quack! Quack! So do the birds!

And so do the ants!
Munch! Munch!
"Everybody loves picnics!"
cries Peppa.

Peppa Plays Football

It's a sunny day and Peppa Pig and
Suzy Sheep are playing tennis.
"To you, Suzy!" cheers Peppa, hitting
the ball. Now, it's Suzy's turn.
"To you, Peppa!" she cries, hitting the ball
straight over Peppa's head. Oh dear!

"Waaaa!" George feels a bit left out.

"Sorry, George," says Peppa. "You can't play tennis. We only have two racquets."

"George can be the ball boy!" cheers Suzy.

"Being a ball boy is a very important job, George," says Peppa.

Peppa and Suzy are having lots of fun,
but they keep missing the ball.
"Ball boy!" they shout together.
"Huff, puff!" George is not having fun.
He keeps running to get the ball and
he is very tired!

"Hello, everyone," cries Peppa when her friends arrive. "We're playing tennis."

"Can we play too?" asks Danny Dog.

"There aren't enough racquets," replies Suzy Sheep.

56

"Let's play football then," says Danny Dog. "Football! Hooray!" everyone cheers.

"We can play girls against boys," says Peppa.

"Each team needs a goalkeeper," says Danny Dog.

"Me, me!" shouts Pedro Pony.

"Me, me!" cries Rebecca Rabbit.

Pedro Pony and Rebecca Rabbit
decide to be the goalkeepers.
"The boys' team will start!" says Danny Dog.
Richard Rabbit gets the ball and runs
very fast, right by Peppa Pig,
Suzy Sheep and Candy Cat
and straight up to the . . .

. . . "GOAL!" cry Danny and Pedro together, as Richard Rabbit kicks the ball straight past Rebecca Rabbit and into the net.
"The boy is a winner!" cheers Danny Dog.
"That's not fair, we weren't ready," moans Peppa.

Rebecca Rabbit picks up the ball and runs.

"Hey!" shouts Danny Dog.

"That's cheating! You can't hold the ball."

"Yes I can!" says Rebecca. "I'm the goalkeeper."

Rebecca throws the ball into the goal,

straight past Pedro Pony.

"GOAL!" she cries.

"That goal is not allowed," says Pedro.

"Yes, it is," says Peppa.

"No, it isn't!" barks Danny.

"What a lot of noise," snorts Daddy Pig.

"I'll be the referee. The next team to get a goal will win the game."

Richard Rabbit and George run off with the football, while everyone is still talking.

"Where's the ball?" asks Peppa.

But it's too late! Richard Rabbit kicks the ball straight into the goal, past Pedro Pony.

"Hooray! The boys win!" cries Danny.

"Football is a silly game," sighs Peppa, disappointed.
"Just a moment," says Daddy Pig. "The boys scored in their own goal, that means the girls win!"
"Really?" gasp all the girls. "Hooray!"
"Football is a great game!" cheers Peppa.
"Ha, ha, ha!" everyone laughs.

Peppa Pig™

School Bus Trip

Peppa and her friends are going on a school bus trip. "Let's check you are all here," says Madame Gazelle. "Here!" cries Peppa.

Woof!

74

Baaa! Grunt! Snort!

"Today," begins Madame Gazelle, "we are going on a trip to the mountains!"

"Hooray!"
cheer all the children.

Peppa and Suzy are
already a little hungry.
"Please can we eat our lunch now?"
they ask Madame Gazelle.

78

"Why not eat your apples and save the rest for the picnic?" she replies. Crunch! Crunch!

The bus has arrived at the foot of the mountain. The road is very steep! "Come on bus! You can make it!" everyone cheers.

Peppa and her friends have
finally made it to the top
of the mountain.

"Look at the view!" gasps Madame Gazelle. All the children look out over the valley.

"Wow!" sighs Peppa, loudly.
"Wow! Wow! Wow!" Peppa hears
in the distance.
"What was that?" she asks quietly.
"It's your echo, Peppa!"
replies Madame Gazelle.

"An echo is the sound you hear when you speak loudly in the mountains," explains Madame Gazelle.
Grunt! Woof! Baaa! Snort!

Snort!
Grunt! Baaa!
Woof!

Now it's time for a picnic lunch.
Peppa loves picnics. Everyone loves
picnics! Munch! Slurp! Munch!
Yum! Yum!

"Where are the ducks?" asks Peppa, taking a bite of her sandwich. "They always turn up when we have picnics."

Quack! Quack! Quack!
Here come the ducks.
"Hello! Would you like some bread?"
Peppa asks them. The ducks are very
lucky today. There is plenty of bread!

The bus has arrived.
It's time to go home.
"Let's all sing a song!" suggests
Madame Gazelle. Hooray!
Everyone has had a great day!

94

Peppa Pig™

Peppa Goes Swimming

It's a lovely sunny day and Peppa and her family are at the swimming pool. "Peppa! George! Let Daddy put on your armbands," snorts Mummy Pig.

Today is George's first time at the pool and he's a bit scared of getting in.

"Why don't you just put one foot in the water?" suggests Daddy Pig.
"Maybe George should try both feet at the same time?" says Mummy Pig.

Splash! Mummy Pig convinces George to jump into the water and he loves it! "Grunt! Hee! Hee! Snort!" shouts George, happily. "Ho! Ho! Well done, George!" snorts Daddy Pig.

Here is Rebecca Rabbit with her brother, Richard and their mummy.

"Hello, everyone!" cries Rebecca.
"Squeak, squeak," says Richard.

"Richard, hold on to this float and you can practise kicking your legs," says Mummy Rabbit.
"George, would you like to try kicking your legs?" asks Mummy Pig.
"Hee! Hee! Float! Snort!" giggles George.

"Big children are very good at swimming," snorts Peppa. "When George and Richard are older, they'll be able to swim like us, won't they, Rebecca?"

"Yes!" says Rebecca, as she watches the boys kicking.

Peppa and Rebecca race each other up and down the pool with their armbands on.

They are having lots of fun swimming and splashing in the water.

Oops! Richard has dropped his toy watering can into the pool. "Mummy! Wah!" cries Richard. "Sorry, Richard, I can't reach. It's too far down," says Mummy Rabbit. Luckily, Daddy Pig is an excellent swimmer. He takes off his glasses and dives down to get it.

"Ho! Ho! There you go!"
snorts Daddy Pig.
"Squeak, squeak!" says Richard.

"Well done, Daddy!" smiles Mummy Pig.

Oh dear! Now Richard is soaking Daddy Pig with the watering can. What a naughty Rabbit! "Hee! Hee! Hee!" George thinks it's hilarious. Everyone has had a wonderful day at the pool!

Peppa Goes Camping

Today, Peppa and George are very excited.

They are going on holiday!

Daddy Pig has a surprise. Honk, honk!

"It's a camper van," grunts Daddy Pig.

"Wow!" gasp Peppa and George.

"We're going on holiday!" sings Peppa. "We're going on holiday, in our camper van! Snort!"

"Hmmm," says Daddy Pig, looking at the map.

"Daddy Pig!" cries Mummy Pig. "Are we lost?"

"Well, er," begins Daddy Pig, "yes!"

Granddad Dog and Danny Dog arrive. "Hello," calls out Peppa. "We're lost!"

"Lost?" asks Granddad Dog, confused.
"Is your satnav broken?"
Peppa, George, Mummy and Daddy Pig
don't know what satnav is.

"Satnav is a computer that helps you find your way," explains Granddad Dog. "Welcome to the car of the future," bleeps the satnav.

"Can you tell us where to go?" asks Peppa.

"Go straight," replies the satnav.

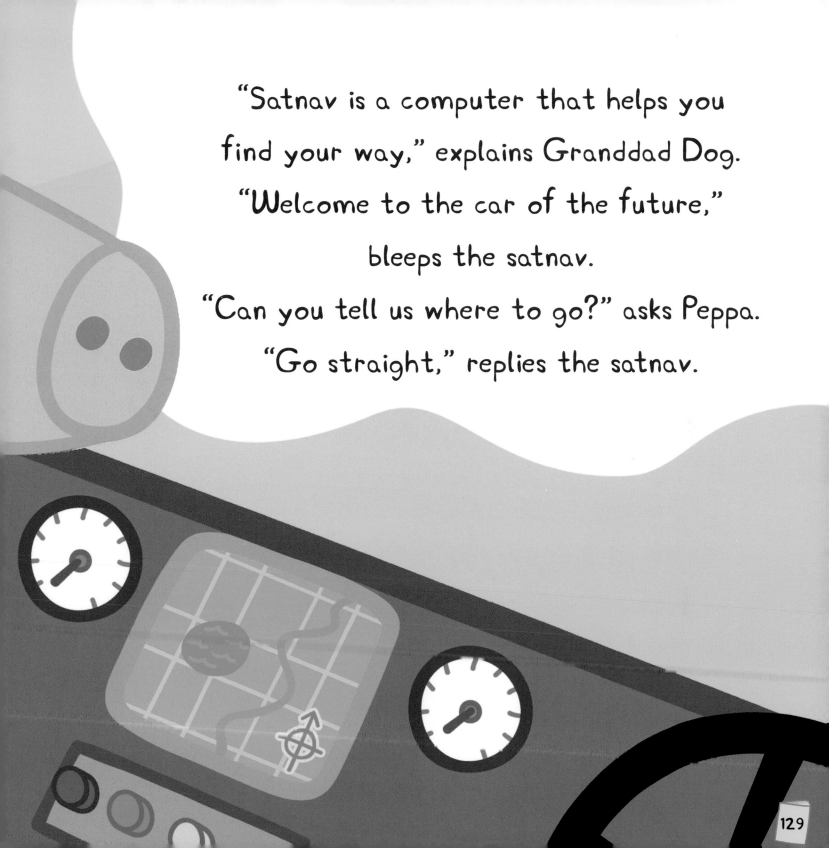

Daddy Pig thanks Granddad Dog
and the family continue on their way.
"We're going on holiday," sings Peppa.
"We're going on holiday, in our camper van!"
Suddenly, the camper van is low on oil.
But Daddy Pig can't find the engine!

Mummy Sheep and Suzy Sheep arrive in their car.
"Hello, Suzy," cries Peppa. "We've lost our engine!"
"Lost your engine?" replies Mummy Sheep.
"I don't know a thing about engines,"
says Mummy Sheep. "But I'll have a look."

"I'm probably wrong, but this looks like an engine," says Mummy Sheep, lifting the boot. "Well spotted, Mummy Sheep," gasps Daddy Pig, pouring oil into the engine. Glug, glug! Daddy Pig thanks Mummy Sheep and the family are off again!

"Are we nearly there yet?" asks Peppa, sighing.

"Just up the next hill," says the satnav.

"You have reached your destination," says the satnav when they get to the top of a steep hill.

"Hooray!" everyone cheers.

"Time for bed," says Mummy Pig.

Peppa and George put on their pyjamas.

"But where will we sleep?" asks Peppa.

"Mummy Pig and I will sleep on this bed,"

says Daddy Pig, pressing a button.

Whirrr!

"Ta-da! A lovely big bed appears in the room.

"And you two will sleep upstairs like you always do," says Mummy Pig.

"Watch this," says Daddy Pig, pressing another button.

Whirrr! Click . . .

Suddenly, the camper van's roof lifts up and a bunk bed appears. Daddy Pig tucks Peppa and George into bed.

"The camper van is just like our little house!" says Peppa.

"Goodnight, everyone," says the satnav. "Sleep well!"

Snore!

Snore!

Snore!

Snore!